THE MAN IN THE MOON AND THE HOT AIR BALLOON

First Marlowe & Company edition, 1996

Published in the United States by
Marlowe & Company
632 Broadway, Seventh Floor
New York, New York 10012

First published by Dragon's World Ltd, 1995

Library of Congress Cataloging - in - Publication Data.

Delamare, David
    The man in the moon and the hot air balloon / David Delamare. --
1st Marlowe & Co. ed.
        p. cm.
    Summary: Winston Smith, a sheep, and Sebastian Curruso, a lion,
build a hot air balloon and set out through the wonders of the night
sky to find out why the Moon has disappeared.
    ISBN 1-56924-832-X
    (1. Moon--Fiction. 2. Hot air balloons--Fiction. 3. Animals-
-Fiction. 4. Stories in rhyme.) I. Title.
PZ8.3.D367Man 1996
[E]--dc20   95-40042
                                                                CIP
                                                                 AC

Typeset by Dragon's World Ltd in ITC Century.
Printed in Italy

THE MAN IN THE MOON AND THE HOT AIR BALLOON

DAVID DELAMARE

MARLOWE & COMPANY
NEW YORK

In London town, long years ago,
Old Winston Smith did dwell.
A player of the violin,
Astronomer as well.

One morning, thumbing through the news,
He read with some dismay
The headline in the largest type:
'THE MOON HAS GONE AWAY.'

So Winston waited for the dusk
Then pulled the curtains wide.
He checked his charts – the time was right
But the Moon had gone to hide.

As weeks passed by he watched the sky
And hoped with all his might
For crescent, half or waning Moon,
But the Moon was not in sight.

4

'This can't go on,' he said aloud.
'Something must be done.'
So he kept awake throughout the night
Hoping an idea would come.

At last, as dawn rose in the sky,
He sprang up from his chair.
'I know,' he cried, 'I'll build a ship
To sail into the air.

'An air balloon with steam and fire
Will carry us past the stars.
We'll land upon the Moon and then
The solution will be ours.'

'I'll need some help, of course,' he said,
'And I know just the man.
Sebastian K. Curruso
Will help me with my plan.'

Together, working day and night,
The vessel for the trip
Took shape, from what was once in part
An old abandoned ship.

They hammered on a garden shed
That came from down the path.
They bolted on a steam device
That heated Winston's bath.

They sewed the mighty air balloon
In purples, browns and reds
With pantaloons and sealing wax
And sheets from Winston's bed.

The work was finally finished
And was such a beautiful sight
That they called the ship *Polaris*
After the star with the brightest light.

The gears were set, the flame was lit,
It burned so bright and red.
'We're off the ground,' Sebastian cried.
'Straight up, full steam ahead!'

The ship, it creaked and groaned a bit
As it rose into the air.
It brushed against the tree tops
Making people point and stare.

Then from a window down below
Came a harsh, indignant cry:
'Why do you have to waste your time
With ventures in the sky?

'So the moonlight's gone! Don't make a fuss.
Nobody really cares.
There's nothing magic about the moon,
It's just a big rock in the air!'

The adventurers took no notice.
They had better things to do.
They checked their map and compass,
And tightened a rope or two.

Sebastian climbed the rigging,
Charting out the course proposed.
The Earth below, all wrapped in clouds,
Grew smaller as they rose.

As Winston occupied himself
With charts and maps galore,
A whoosh was heard. It sounded like
A mighty ocean roar!

He stood and leaned out over the rail
And saw, as though in a race,
A meteor go speeding by
Which knocked him into space.

Poor Winston tumbled down and down,
His feet flew by his face.
His glasses and his hat passed by
Like runners in a race.

His tummy became queasy.
He was sure he'd lost a shoe.
And, from far above, Sebastian
Was fading out of view.

Then looking down, as he tumbled and turned,
He saw a gleam amid the blackness.
'Aha,' he cried, 'I can save myself
If I'm bold but not too reckless.'

He stretched as far as he could stretch,
Which wasn't very far,
But luck was his, and he found that he
Was hanging from a star.

He caught his glasses and his hat
As they went whistling by.
He kept a grip as best he could
Suspended in the sky.

His arm reached out to catch the shoe,
Straining for all he was worth,
But he could not quite grasp it
As it descended to the Earth.

Then up above he heard the sound
Of steam machines and fire.
'I'll rescue you,' Sebastian called.
'Before both your arms tire.'

Sebastian quickly grabbed the anchor
And tied it to a rope.
Slow but sure he lowered it down
To Winston's reaching grope.

18

Sebastian hoisted Winston up
And secured him on the ship.
He gave him some replacement shoes
To help him on the trip.

He made him tea and buttered toast
And sat him in a chair.
'You rest a bit, my dear old friend,
For we will soon be there.'

Then came a drip, a splash, a stream,
Cascading sheets of white.
'The Milky Way,' Sebastian cried,
'A waterfall of light!'

The ship passed through the milky falls
And on the other side
A galaxy of constellations
Played before their eyes.

'We're near the Moon,' Sebastian said.
'It's very close, I know.'
He called out to the archer
And the archer drew his bow.

He fired off an arrow
That exploded like a rocket.
'Just follow that and you'll soon have
Some moonstones in your pocket.'

The swiftly flying arrow
Streamed out its star dust tail
And led the bold adventurers
As sure as any trail.

They scrambled down the ladder
And reached the ground below.
'That castle with its telescope
Must be where we need to go.'

24

They entered through the grandest arch
With cherubs carved in stone.
Said Winston rather nervously,
'Perhaps there's no one home.'

They tip-toed down a corridor
Then turned around a bend
To see a face, all framed in stars.
They'd reached their journey's end.

The Moon looked sad and miserable,
A tear ran down his cheek.
He did not greet or welcome them,
He did not smile or speak.

Sebastian stepped up to him,
And bowed politely low.
'Dear Moon,' he said. 'To Earth you're dark,
Please tell us why that's so.'

Man in the Moon spoke quietly.
They listened with delight.
'For Earth, the Moon no longer is
A grand and wondrous sight.

'From here I watch the world below
And to my great dismay,
I see the magic of the Moon
Has slowly slipped away.'

Then from his case, old Winston drew
An instrument so dear.
'Sir, if I may, I'd like to play
A song that you should hear.'

So Winston played the man a song
Written about the Moon.
The Moon began to beam with light;
He really loved the tune.

'If the beauty of that splendid song
By moonlight was inspired,
Then in my heart I feel quite sure
Moonlight *must* be required.'

Those were the last words that they heard
And as they left the ground,
The Moon burst into glorious light
That shimmered all around.

The page one story, printed bold,
Read 'The Moon's light has returned!'
The two explorers, no one else,
Knew why the moonlight burned.

But the story Winston most enjoyed
Which brought a smile to his face
Was: 'A bull reports being hit
By a Shoe from Outer Space.'

THE END